HENRY'S *BUSY* DAY

WITHDRAWN

Rod Campbell

VIKING KESTREL

This is Henry.

He **never** sits still!

He likes to

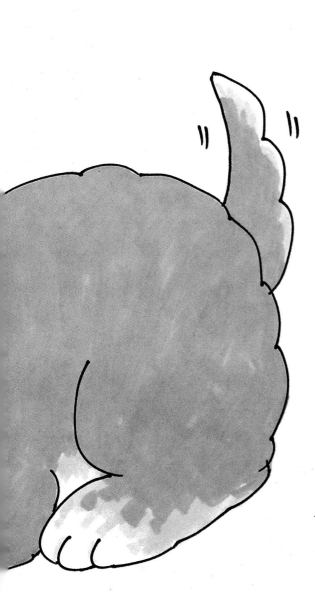

chew my slippers.

He likes to

scratch his back.

He likes to

chase the pigeons.

He likes to

dig a hole.

He likes to

bark at the cat.

He likes to

swim in the pond.

He likes to

play with his friends.

After such a
busy day,
Henry likes to